MW01064643

"To my children and grandchildren."

Throughout our lives, outside of faith and family, nothing is more important than our values. Values are not something you can see or reach out and touch, but something that we live by, something that we demonstrate in our daily lives that defines the person we are. Although there are many more, we have selected these 16 core/intrinsic values (Goals for Success) for our Kansas State University football program.

These values, when brought into our lives daily and lived by faithfully, will indeed bring us the greatest opportunity for success in all areas of our lives and certainly nothing that our parents and family members haven't attempted to teach us throughout our young lives. So many players from our football program over the past 25 years have written me or shared with me personally how important our 16 Goals (core values) have been for them and that they have had great successes in their lives, be it with their faith, their family, their education, athletics, their careers, or in their own personal lives. It sounds easy, but it can be difficult if we allow it to be.

Just knowing the Goal (core value) will not bring us the successes we desire, but living it day to day, that Goal certainly will.

Bill Snyder

© 2017 Kraken Books
Text © Bill Snyder
with Jefferson Knapp
Illustrations © Tim Ladwig

Published and produced by
Kraken Books Ltd.
1019 Skyview Drive
El Dorado, KS 67042

For more information on this book,
please check out
www.krakenbooks.com

ISBN 978-0-9969742-1-9

Printed in United State of America through
Bolton Associates, Inc. Grass Valley, CA 95945

10 9 8 7 6 5 4 3 2 1

KRAKEN
BOOKS
Ltd.

"What's good *is good
for everyone. What's* right
is right for everyone*."*

COACH BILL SNYDER

TAKE IT FROM ME

WITH JEFFERSON KNAPP

Have you ever wanted something so badly, but
didn't know how to reach it?
Thought you weren't good enough, but
dreamed you could achieve it?
Then take my advice and pay heed to these words.
These sixteen goals should forever be heard….

1 COMMITMENT

It's easy to quit when losing.
High **expectations** can be hard.
Focus your mind, dedicate your time,
And winning will be your **reward**.

*"You can achieve all you desire if you are committed to it
and to each of these goals."* Bill Snyder

2 UNSELFISHNESS

Does the glory belong to you?
Did you **do it** all by yourself?
Embrace your teammates and win **together**.
Put that ego on the shelf.

"Be humble—care more about others." Bill Snyder

3 UNITY

There are eleven opponents against you.
You can't **win** when you are alone.
With one you are weak, ten more you are **strong**.
Together you're solid as stone.

"Care about each other." Bill Snyder

4 IMPROVE

Things get tougher as you move along.
Don't settle for where you are.
Build on your strengths, **work** on your weaknesses,
And no doubt you will **go** far.

"Everyday in every part of your life." Bill Snyder

HOME

5 BE TOUGH

How many opponents can knock you down?
How many times can you take a hit?
Make your body strong, as well as your mind.
Be filled with courage and grit.

"Mental toughness/strength makes us stronger." Bill Snyder

6 SELF DISCIPLINE

When you want to do something you shouldn't,
And you know those actions aren't right,
Turn your focus around, plant your feet on firm ground,
And victory will be in sight.

*"Do what is right, the right way and do it that way every time,
and don't accept less."* Bill Snyder

7 GREAT EFFORT

You want to end the game with satisfaction,
Regardless if you **win or lose**.
Whether you stand or fall, you give it your all,
It's up to you to **choose**.

"Your very, very best every time." Bill Snyder

8 ENTHUSIASM

Get excited; the big day is here.
The game is about to start!
Relish the moment, take it all in,
And compete with **joy** in your heart.

"In every area of your life—enjoy the climb." Bill Snyder

PRIDE

9 ELIMINATE MISTAKES

Take an eraser and scrub away the wrong.
Try to never do it again.
When you eliminate mistakes and continue to improve,
That will count as a win.

"The climb to success is much quicker when we correct our mistakes." Bill Snyder

10 NEVER GIVE UP

Never give up; never surrender.
That's the secret to your success.
However much time is left on the clock,
You should always give it your best.

"Never, Never, Never." Bill Snyder

11 DON'T ACCEPT LOSING

Don't accept losing, because when you do,
You settle for failure and strife.
You were born to succeed, so try, try again
And make winning a part of your life.

"Losing is not doing your best. If you give up one time it becomes easier to do it again and again." Bill Snyder

12 NO SELF LIMITATIONS

If you think all you can do is what you've already done,
You need to keep striving for more.
You are a winner and you're not finished.
You've got so much more in store.

"Expect more of yourself." Bill Snyder

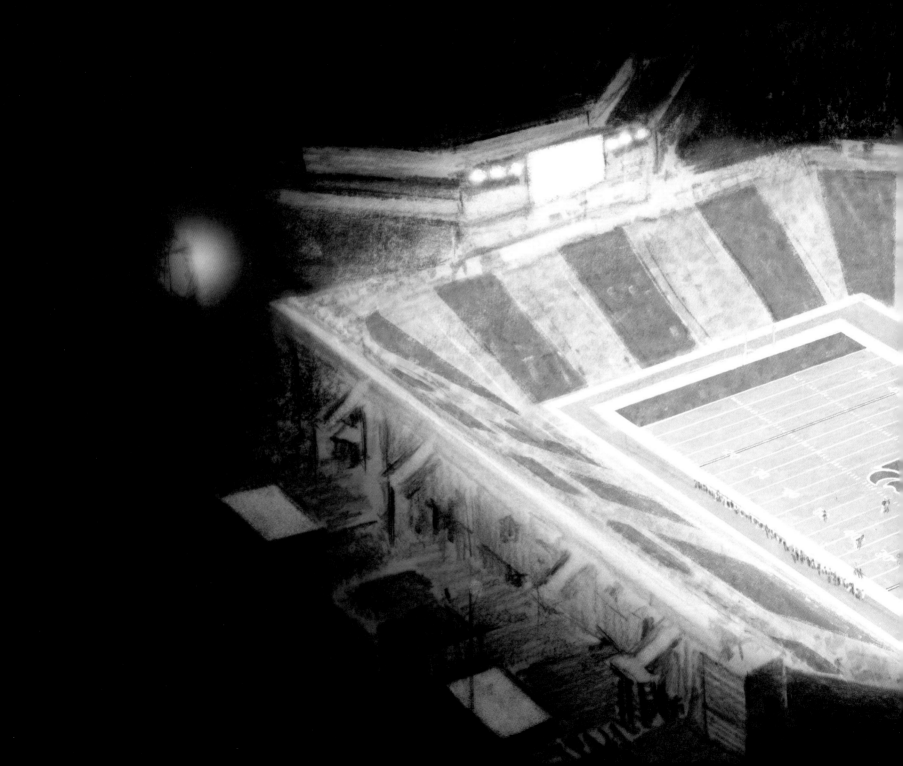

FAMILY

13 EXPECT TO WIN

Expect to win no matter the challenge;
That is the right frame of mind.
With a positive attitude, and a whole lot of heart,
Victory will be easy to find!

"And truly believe you will." Bill Snyder

14 CONSISTENCY

Consistency, consistency!
Keep it constant every day.
If something works, hang onto it.
That is the very best way.

"Your very, very best every time." Bill Snyder

15 LEADERSHIP

Everyone looks up to someone;
It might as well be you.
When challenges arise, step up and lead,
And the rest will follow through.

"Everyone can set a good example." Bill Snyder

16 RESPONSIBILITY

We all like to claim the good stuff,
But it's more important to own up to mistakes.
Your life is determined by your actions.
Don't blame others for the problems you make.

"You are responsible for everything that you do ." Bill Snyder

So if you
Paid attention to these things,
Please keep them
Close to your chest.
I leave with you
my heart, my time & my gratitude,
And my 16 goals for Success.

With love and best wishes
for a wonderful and
Successful life.

Bill Snyder

Love,

Coach Bill Snyder